SUPER BOWL SUPERSTARS

ELI MANNING
and the
New York Giants

SUPER BOWL XLII

by Michael Sandler

Consultant: Norries Wilson
Head Football Coach
Columbia University

BEARPORT PUBLISHING

New York, New York

Credits

Cover and Title Page, © Evan Pinkus/Getty Images; 4, © Andy Lyons/Getty Images; 5, © Andy Lyons/Getty Images; 6, © Patrick Murphy-Racey/Sports Illustrated; 7, © Ronald Martinez/Getty Images; 8, © AP Images/Bill Kostroun; 9, © AP Images/Kathy Willens; 10, © Reuters/Jessica Rinaldi; 11, © Newscom.com; 12, © Tom Hauck/Getty Images; 13, © Jed Jacobsohn/Getty Images; 14, © Chris McGrath/Getty Images; 15, © Elsa/Getty Images; 16, © Paul Spinelli/Getty Images; 17, © Al Tielemans/Sports Illustrated; 18, © Paul Spinelli/Getty Images; 19, © AP Images/Elaine Thompson; 20, © Doug Mills/The New York Times/Redux; 21, © Newscom.com; 22L, © Tom Hauck/Getty Images; 22R, © Scott Boehm/Getty Images.

Publisher: Kenn Goin
Senior Editor: Lisa Wiseman
Creative Director: Spencer Brinker
Design: Deborah Kaiser
Photo Researcher: Jennifer Bright

Library of Congress Cataloging-in-Publication Data

Sandler, Michael, 1965–
 Eli Manning and the New York Giants : Super Bowl XLII / by Michael Sandler.
   p. cm. — (Super bowl superstars)
 Includes bibliographical references and index.
 ISBN-13: 978-1-59716-736-9 (library binding)
 ISBN-10: 1-59716-736-3 (library binding)
 1. Manning, Eli, 1981–2. Football players—New York (State)—Biography—Juvenile literature. 3. New York Giants (Football team)—Biography—Juvenile literature. 4. Super Bowl (42nd : 2008 : University of Phoenix Stadium, Glendale, Ariz.)—Juvenile literature. I. Title.

 GV939.M289S25 2009
 796.332092—dc22
 (B)

                          2008011380

For more information, write to Bearport Publishing Company, Inc., 101 Fifth Avenue, Suite 6R, New York, New York 10003. Printed in the United States of America.

10 9 8 7 6 5 4 3 2 1

★ Contents ★

Eli Under Pressure

The New England Patriots' **defenders** were everywhere. They charged at New York Giants quarterback Eli Manning. They surrounded and grabbed him. The young quarterback seemed lost. He was sinking in a sea of New England players.

Eli had to get away from the Patriots. His team was losing with only a minute left to play in Super Bowl XLII (42). If Eli got **sacked**, New York's championship dreams would die. "All I was trying to do was escape," Eli said later. "…And then I saw Tyree."

Fans cheering on the Giants during Super Bowl XLII (42) on February 3, 2008

4

Eli (#10) tries to break free from the Patriots' players.

New York was trying for its third Super Bowl win. The Giants had won twice before, in 1987 and 1991.

Growing Up with the Game

Eli Manning grew up in a famous football family. His father, Archie Manning, had played for the New Orleans Saints in the 1970s and 1980s. His older brothers, Cooper and Peyton, were also football players. Peyton became a **pro** quarterback just like his dad.

Eli was the baby of the family. Not surprisingly, he loved football just like the rest of the Mannings. He became a top quarterback in high school and later at the University of Mississippi.

Eli (right) and his big brother
Peyton (left) in 1996

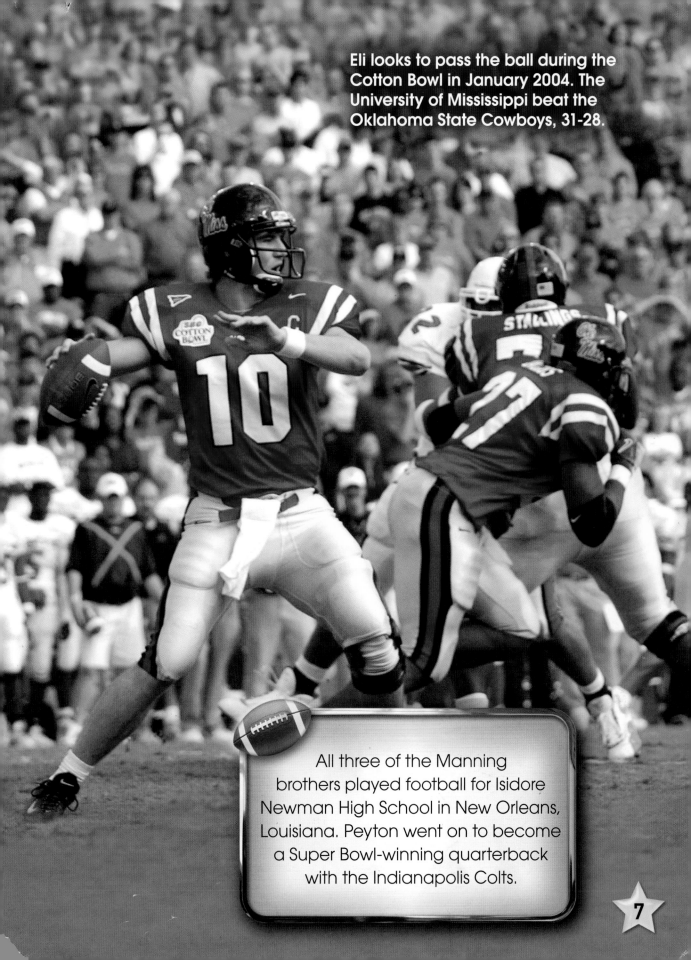

Eli looks to pass the ball during the Cotton Bowl in January 2004. The University of Mississippi beat the Oklahoma State Cowboys, 31-28.

All three of the Manning brothers played football for Isidore Newman High School in New Orleans, Louisiana. Peyton went on to become a Super Bowl-winning quarterback with the Indianapolis Colts.

Joining the Giants

Eli joined the Giants in 2004 after a great college career. New York fans were thrilled. They wondered if Eli would be able to lead the team to its first Super Bowl win since 1991.

Getting that win wouldn't be easy, though. Eli's first years were tough. The Giants were a good team, but not a great one. In both 2005 and 2006 they made the **playoffs**, but they didn't go any further.

The playoff losses made some fans question Eli's **leadership**. He made too many **turnovers**, they said. Unlike his older brother Peyton, he didn't win big games.

Eli (center) holds up his Giants jersey.

A disappointed Eli during the playoffs in 2006

Eli was the first player chosen in the 2004 National Football League (NFL) **draft**.

Turning It Around

The 2007 season started off poorly with the Giants losing their first two games. Fans continued grumbling about Eli.

Eli didn't lose his confidence, though. Neither did his teammates or the Giants' coach, Tom Coughlin. He believed in Eli and the team. "I think we're a better football team than we've shown," he said.

Coach Coughlin was right. New York won their next six games. Then, in the playoffs, Eli guided the Giants to big wins over the Tampa Bay Buccaneers and the Dallas Cowboys.

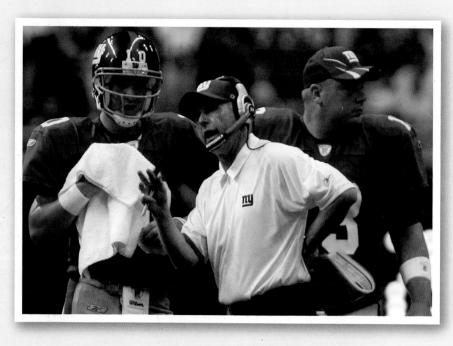

Giants coach Tom Coughlin (center) talks with Eli (left) on the sidelines.

Running back Ahmad Bradshaw (#44) played a big role in New York's playoff success.

In each playoff game, the Giants had to play on their **opponent's** home field. It didn't bother the Giants, however. In 2007–2008, they set an NFL record by winning ten road games in a row.

Conquering the Cold

Next the Giants traveled to Green Bay, Wisconsin, to play the Packers in the **NFC Championship Game**. The weather in Wisconsin was unbelievably cold on game day. The **wind chill** was –20° F (–28° C). The grass field was as hard as concrete. The frozen ball felt like a rock.

The Packers were used to playing in icy conditions. The Giants proved to be the tougher cold-weather team, however. Eli led two come-from-behind **drives** on the way to a 23-20 **overtime** win. The Giants were headed to Super Bowl XLII (42)!

Eli wore a special red glove to help grip the frozen football.

Lawrence Tynes's (#9) game-winning field goal sent New York to the Super Bowl.

The weather during the game played in Green Bay was the coldest in the history of the New York Giants.

The Patriots

Even though they defeated the Packers, few people thought the Giants would beat their Super Bowl opponents, the New England Patriots. The Patriots were more than just a good team—they were probably the best in NFL history.

Led by quarterback Tom Brady and **receiver** Randy Moss, New England hadn't lost a game all year. Counting their two playoff victories, they were 18-0. Football fans everywhere expected Tom and the Patriots to easily win the Super Bowl and complete a perfect season.

The Patriots celebrate their 18th straight victory.

Quarterback Tom Brady was the NFL's Most Valuable Player (MVP) in 2007. He had led New England to victory in three of the last six Super Bowls.

The 1972 Miami Dolphins were the only team in NFL history to go **undefeated** in a season and win a Super Bowl.

Back and Forth

During the game, the Giants surprised nearly everyone and kept the score close. Eli took his time on long drives. The slow **pace** kept New England's dangerous offense off the field.

When the Patriots did have the ball, New York's defense hounded Tom Brady. He barely had time to throw passes. Again and again, he was hurled to the ground.

Then, in the fourth quarter, New York grabbed the lead. Suddenly, New England realized they just might lose the game.

With his perfect season at risk, Tom struck back. An 80-yard (73-m) touchdown drive pushed New England ahead, 14-10. Now it was the Giants' turn to be nervous.

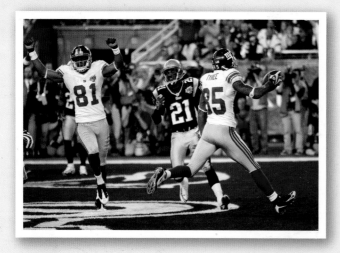

Eli's fourth-quarter pass to David Tyree (#85) gave New York a 10-7 lead.

Michael Strahan (left) made things hard for Patriots quarterback Tom Brady (right).

Tom Brady was sacked five times. Michael Strahan, Kawika Mitchell, and Jay Alford each had one sack, while Justin Tuck had two.

A Promise

Eli tried to calm his teammates. "Don't worry," he said. "We're going to win this game."

Could Eli keep his promise? Two quick passes to receiver Amani Toomer gained New York some yards. With just 1:15 minutes left, however, the Giants were still a long way from the **end zone**.

Then Eli dropped back again. This time four Patriots charged at him. A **devastating** sack seemed certain.

Somehow, though, Eli got away. He launched a pass deep downfield. Receiver David Tyree jumped up to catch it. He tumbled to the ground, trapping the ball against his helmet.

Eli was able to break free from the Patriots.

"I wouldn't let it go," said David Tyree (#85) about his catch.

Before the Super Bowl, David Tyree had caught only five passes all year.

19

Plaxico's Play

No one could believe it. Eli hadn't been sacked! David had made the catch! The Giants were just 24 yards (22 m) from the end zone.

Four plays later, Eli came through again. He spotted Plaxico Burress heading down the field. He threw the ball high and fast toward the Giants' top receiver. Plaxico reached up and pulled the ball down in the corner of the end zone. Touchdown! The Giants took a 17-14 lead.

It was all New York needed. They had defeated the mighty Patriots in the biggest Super Bowl upset ever. Eli and the Giants were champions!

Plaxico Burress scores the game-winning touchdown.

Eli (#10) and running back Brandon Jacobs (#27) celebrate the Giants' victory.

After the game, Eli was named MVP of Super Bowl XLII (42), just like his brother Peyton had been named MVP the year before in Super Bowl XLI (41).

★ Key Players ★

There were other key players
on the New York Giants who helped win
Super Bowl XLII (42). Here are two of them.

★ David Tyree #85

Position	Wide Receiver
Born	1/3/1980 in Livingston, New Jersey
Height	6' 0" (1.83 m)
Weight	206 pounds (93 kg)
Key Plays	Caught a five-yard (5-m) touchdown pass from Eli Manning; made the most important catch on the Giants' final drive

★ Justin Tuck #91

Position	Defensive End
Born	3/29/1983 in Kellyton, Alabama
Height	6' 5" (1.96 m)
Weight	274 pounds (124 kg)
Key Plays	Sacked New England quarterback Tom Brady twice and forced a Patriots fumble

★ Glossary ★

defenders (di-FEN-durz)
players who have the job of trying to stop the other team from scoring

devastating (DEV-uh-*stay*-ting)
damaging, very upsetting

draft (DRAFT)
an event in which NFL teams choose college players to be on their teams

drives (DRIVEZ)
series of plays in which the team with the ball tries to move down the field

end zone (END ZOHN)
the area at either end of a football field where touchdowns are scored

leadership (LEED-ur-ship)
the ability to guide and inspire other players

NFC Championship Game
(EN EFF SEE CHAM-pee-uhn-*ship* GAME) a playoff game that decides which National Football Conference (NFC) team will go to the Super Bowl

opponent (uh-POH-nuhnt)
a team that another team plays against in a sporting event

overtime (OH-vur-*time*)
extra playing time added to a game when the score remains tied after four quarters of play

pace (PAYSS)
the speed at which someone does something

playoffs (PLAY-awfss)
the games held after the end of the regular season that determine the NFL's champion

pro (PROH)
short for "professional"; a person who is paid to play a sport

receiver (ri-SEE-vur)
a player whose job it is to catch passes

sacked (SAKT)
when a quarterback is tackled behind the line of scrimmage while attempting to throw a pass

turnovers (TURN-*oh*-vurz)
plays that result in the loss of the football to the other team

undefeated (UHN-duh-*feet*-id)
not having lost a single game

wind chill (WIND CHIL)
a measurement of temperature and wind speed that shows how cold people will feel when they're outside

Bibliography

The Daily News (New York)

The New York Times

Sports Illustrated

NFL.com

Read More

Diprimio, Pete. *Eli Manning.* Childs, MD: Mitchell Lane Publishers (2008).

Polzer, Tim. *Super Bowl Stories.* New York: Scholastic (2007).

Stewart, Mark. *The New York Giants (Team Spirit).* Chicago, Il: Norwood House Press (2007).

Learn More Online

To learn more about Eli Manning,
the New York Giants, and the Super Bowl, visit
www.bearportpublishing.com/SuperBowlSuperstars

Index